MY PRAIRIE CHRISTMAS

by Brett Harvey

illustrations by Deborah Kogan Ray

Holiday House/New York

Text copyright © 1990 by Brett Harvey
Illustrations copyright © 1990 by Deborah Kogan Ray
All rights reserved
Printed in the United States of America
First Edition

Library of Congress Cataloging-in-Publication Data

Harvey, Brett.
My prairie Christmas / written by Brett Harvey ;
illustrated by Deborah Kogan Ray. — 1st ed.
p.   cm.
Summary: On the first Christmas after Eleanor's family
moves to a house on the prairie,
everyone becomes worried when
Papa goes out to cut down a Christmas tree
and does not come back.
ISBN 0-8234-0827-2
[1. Christmas—Fiction.   2. Frontier and pioneer life—Fiction.
3. West (U.S.)—Fiction.j.]   I. Ray, Deborah Kogan, 1940–   ill.
II. Title.
PZ7.H26747Mx   1990
[E]—dc20   90-55104   CIP   AC
ISBN 0-8234-0827-2

Along about November, I started to worry about Christmas. It was our first year on the prairie and everything here was so different from where we'd come from. Back home in Maine, Christmas was my favorite time. Mama and Papa, my sister Marjorie, my baby brother Billy and I got together with our relatives at Aunt Addie's house. There was special, delicious food and presents for everyone. But best of all was our tree, a big, green pine tree that Papa and I cut down in the woods near our house. Ah, how beautiful it was after we decorated it with shiny, tin ornaments and strings of red cranberries. There was a delicious smell of scorching pine needles as Papa walked around the tree and lit the candles.

I loved our new home on the prairie, sitting in the middle of its ocean of grass. But how would we celebrate Christmas? All our relatives were too far away to come and there wasn't much to eat except corn. And where would we ever get a tree? There were no trees nearby except the cottonwoods in the river bottom. Whenever I asked Papa about a tree, he said, "Don't worry, Rabbit, we'll have one. I saw a grove of nice cedars outside of Britton. When the time comes, we'll go out and cut one of them." But what would we put on our tree? There were no cranberries on the prairie, and we'd left our box of shiny ornaments back in Maine.

One day Mama announced, "We'd better get started making our decorations or we won't have anything to put on our tree." I couldn't imagine what we'd make, but Mama had good ideas. She showed us how to twist cornhusks that she had dyed into little dolls. Marjorie and I even tried twisting them into prairie dogs and jackrabbits. After we had a big pile of decorations, we popped corn and strung yards of popcorn.

By December, the days had turned cold and dark and we had to spend more time indoors. It was hard to hide the presents I was making because our house was so tiny. Every day I worked on a book for Mama with pictures of things I knew she missed: maple trees, rosebushes, a shop with hats in the window. For Marjorie I was sewing a pillow stuffed with silky cottonwood seeds. Mama was helping Marjorie and me sew a warm scarf for Papa out of scraps of material. She was also helping me make a stuffed rabbit for Billy. We filled it with corn kernels till it looked nice and plump.

Two days before Christmas, I woke in the night to the wind howling so loud and lonely I thought it was wolves. The next morning the sky was thick and milky-white as if we were sitting in the middle of a cloud. Papa stood looking out the window and said, "I'd better go get that tree before the snow starts." I opened my mouth to ask if I could come, but before I even got the words out Papa said, "No, Rabbit, I think we're in for a blizzard and I need you to stay here with Mama."

After Papa left, Mama said, "We'd better see what kind of Christmas baking we can do with corn. Let's see . . . we have molasses, milk, butter, and eggs. We can make Indian pudding. I know it isn't Christmas cookies, but it's sweet and special. Elenore, run out to the barn and get me two good eggs."

While Mama and I worked on the pudding, Marjorie kept Billy out of our way by playing with him on the floor. Suddenly she looked up and said, "Mama, I can't see anything out the window." The snow was coming down so hard it looked like a thick white curtain. We ran to the window and tried to see through the snow, but we couldn't even find the barn. Mama looked at me and said, "Don't worry, Rabbit, Papa will be fine." But there was a little line between her eyebrows that told me she was worried, too.

By suppertime Papa still wasn't back. I didn't care about the tree anymore if only Papa would come home. What if something bad had happened to him?

After dinner, Mama sat in her rocker and called us to her. "Now listen, children," she said in a wobbly voice. "Even if Papa isn't here, we're having Christmas. Tonight, I'll tell you the Christmas story, just as I always do. And when you wake in the morning, there will be Papa and there will be a tree." Then she told us the story of the baby Jesus and the star and the wise men and the shepherds. By the time she had finished, Marjorie and Billy were both asleep. "Do you really think Papa will be here?" I whispered as Mama tucked us in. "Rabbit, I can't promise," she said. "All I can tell you is I feel so sure he will be."

When I woke up the next morning, the house was cold and still. After a moment, I realized the wind had stopped. There were ice crystals on the windows that looked like diamonds in the sunlight. Then I remembered it was Christmas Day. Then I remembered about Papa. I lay in bed, listening hard for his voice or his snore. The chink of the stove lid told me someone was up and starting the fire. I tiptoed across the cold floor and peeked into the front room. Mama was feeding buffalo chips into the stove. There was no sign of Papa. When Mama turned to me, her eyes looked red and swollen. I ran to her and buried my face in her skirt. After a while she said quietly, "It's still Christmas, Elenore. Go wake your sister and brother and get dressed."

After breakfast Mama said, "We can't have Christmas without a tree. We'll just have to go get ourselves a cottonwood from the river bottom." We pulled on our boots and coats and wrapped ourselves in our scarves. We put Billy in a sling on Mama's back, like an Indian baby. Mama got Papa's ax down from the wall and we started out. Outside, the wind had blown the snow into huge drifts, but there were other places where the snow wasn't that deep. Marjorie and I went first to make a path for Mama. The sun sparkled on the snow and it felt good to be outside after so long. I almost forgot to worry about Papa.

At the river bottom we found a young cottonwood that was just the right size, and Mama chopped it down. I was surprised she could use the ax as well as Papa. Going back wasn't so easy. The little tree was hard to drag up the riverbank and through the snow, even with Marjorie and I carrying the trunk and Mama holding the top.

Back home the cottonwood looked scrawny and sad, not at all like our big, green tree back in Maine. But Mama made us get right to work stringing the popcorn chains around the tree and hanging our cornhusk dolls from the naked branches. The tree was beginning to look better, but it still seemed unfinished. Then Mama had an idea. She brought out her bag of cottonwood silk and we spread it on the branches. "There," said Mama, stepping back to look at the tree, "that's much better!"

Suddenly we heard a sound outside. The door burst open and there was Papa! We all screamed and flew at him so hard we almost knocked him down. "Whoa, there everybody," he said, laughing, and then he saw the tree. "Well well," he said, "I guess it's a good thing I didn't bring another tree, isn't it? But look what I *did* bring," he added. "Here's our Christmas barrel from Aunt Addie."

Later Papa told us how the snowstorm had caught him just outside of Britton, how he'd made it as far as the post office where he'd found Aunt Addie's barrel, and how the blizzard was so bad he and two other men had to spend the night in the post office. "By this morning I knew you'd be so worried about me I didn't want to take the time to go out and cut a tree, so I just borrowed the postmaster's sled, loaded up the barrel, and came home as fast as I could."

It was a wonderful Christmas after all. Mama had made us soft flannel nightgowns. Papa had made us a cottonwood crêche and rubbed it with dirt until it was soft as silk. He'd fashioned the Christmas story figures out of clay from the river bottom. Aunt Addie's barrel was filled with all sorts of good things. There were little bags of nuts and raisins and two sacks of wheat flour and white sugar. My mouth watered thinking about the delicious cookies and breads we would bake. There were presents for all of us. And at the bottom of the barrel was the old tin star from our Christmas tree in Maine. Mama fixed it to the top of our cottonwood and said, "Now this little tree looks just as nice as any tree we've ever had."

Mama roasted a prairie hen. We ate it with Aunt Addie's special cranberry sauce and with real biscuits made from her wheat flour. Marjorie and Billy were so tired they almost fell into their Indian pudding. I helped Mama and Papa carry them to bed. While Mama tucked them in, Papa said, "Come on, Rabbit, let's have a look at the stars."

We put on our coats and boots and went outside. It was silent except for the sound of our boots breaking through the crust on the snow. Papa and I stood still and looked up, watching our breath making clouds in the icy air. After a while we heard Mama come out and crunch across the snow behind us. Then I felt her hand on my shoulder. There was no moon, only the velvety blue sky and millions of stars like tiny, twinkling diamonds. Suddenly I felt so small it made me shiver.

"Are these stars different from the ones we had back home in Maine?" I whispered.

"No, Rabbit," said Mama. "These are the same stars we had in Maine."

"I guess we can just see more stars out here because there aren't any trees in the way," I said.

As I watched the stars winking in the big, dark sky above us, I felt warm inside on our first prairie Christmas.